I Was There...

ALONE IN THE
TRENCHES

For my late grandad Bertie, who probably met my grandma while he was on army training in Thetford, Suffolk, and who, although he served during the Great War, like many of his generation would never talk about what he saw.

While this book is based on real characters and actual historical events, some situations and people are fictional, created by the author.

Scholastic Children's Books
Euston House,
24 Eversholt Street
London, NW1 1DB, UK

A division of Scholastic Ltd
London ~ New York ~ Toronto ~ Sydney ~ Auckland
Mexico City ~ New Delhi ~ Hong Kong

First published in the UK by Scholastic Ltd, 2014

Text copyright © Vince Cross, 2014

Illustrations by Michael Garton
© Scholastic Ltd, 2014

ISBN 978 1407 14507 5

Printed and bound by CPI Group (UK) Ltd, Croydon, CR0 4YY

1 3 5 7 9 10 8 6 4 2

I Was There...

ALONE IN THE TRENCHES

Vince Cross

CHAPTER ONE

We'd run out of flour at the farm. Again.
At six in the morning Mum was already at
the end of her tether.

"You'll have to go into Ypres. Get enough
bread to last us a couple of days. And as
much flour as you can carry."
It was more than an hour's walk. And
yesterday I'd been sure I'd heard explosions
from the direction of town. "Oh, Mum," I
moaned. "Do I have to? I'm so scared…"

I was lazy as much as frightened.

"Can't you see I've got my hands full?"
she shouted. "I've been up half the night
with Grandma. Don't you think we're all

scared? You'll go and say no more about it if you want to eat today."

I was starting to hate living in the cold farmhouse now that Dad wasn't there to spoil me.

In Ypres the bell on Madame Peyroux's shop door tinkled. She hobbled from the shadows to look me up and down accusingly.

"It's very early. And you're on your own. Where's your mother then? It's far too dangerous for you to come here by yourself."

"Didn't you know?" I answered. "It's just the three of us now. And Mum can't leave Grandma…"

"But what about your father?" she began, and then broke off, realizing she'd put her foot in it.

"I'm not sure," I said miserably. "He disappeared. With Michel. They went out and they didn't come back. It's been a fortnight…"

Madame Peyroux looked uncomfortable. She was probably a bit shocked she hadn't heard any gossip, but I could see she'd misunderstood. She was thinking Dad had just walked out and left us. People were doing stranger things just then.

"I'm so sorry," she said, doing her best to sound as if she meant it. Madame Peyroux didn't look well. Her cheeks had a high colour and her movements were fidgety. Her eyes seemed small and frightened. She shoved two loaves in my hand with a few *centimes* change. "Please send my regards … my sympathy. Tell your mother to let me know if there's anything I can do … if we're still here, that is!"

I couldn't wait to get out of her poky little shop. I'd only known Madame P. a few months, but long enough to dislike her. It would be all over the city before the day was out: "*Poor Madame Martin. I never did trust that man…*" As I shut the door behind me my chest began to heave and tears stung my eyes.

It was a very beautiful, clear November morning. When I'd left at first light, the sky had been a deep, unbroken blue shading into gold behind the silhouettes of the trees on the horizon. A first scattering of winter frost was showing across the deep brown ridges of the ploughed fields, like icing sugar on a chocolate cake. At half past seven the streets and squares of Ypres were still empty of people. Everything was calm and peaceful around the ancient stones of the Cloth Hall and the Cathedral. "*Where is everybody this morning?*" I remember thinking. And then, without warning, came a terrible, monstrous sound that cut the sky in half. It sounded like a cross between the tearing of a sheet and a sudden vicious scatter of rain, but so much louder and more sinister. On its heels was a deafening explosion that shook the ground beneath me. I staggered, and nearly lost balance. A fierce gust of wind and dirt whipped past my face. A shower of plaster from somewhere above fell onto my hair and shoulders. I was terrified and thought that I was about to die.

Suddenly the streets were filled with men and women, heads down, tucking shirts into breeches, wiping their hands on aprons. They were running around shouting and gesturing. They gathered buckets and brooms as if all they had to do was mop up some spilled milk. But as they swept and tidied, a second shell whined in towards the city, and then a third. It was obvious this was no accident or mistake. Ypres wouldn't be put back together today, or tomorrow, or perhaps ever again. The Germans had us in their sights.

"How dare they destroy our beautiful homes!" said one man. "It's downright criminal!"

"Remember what happened in Louvain," retorted another. "The guns didn't leave a building standing or spare a single family. Why should we be any different?"

A church bell started tolling, and then another. An electric alarm bell began to ring somewhere close by and wouldn't stop. In the distance a trumpeter started to play the Belgian national anthem. Horses and carts appeared, as well as one or two motorized lorries. Overhead I began to hear the noise of an aeroplane engine. People in the street looked up anxiously. I could see the 'plane circling out beyond the *Grand Place*. There were two men inside it. One was throwing bombs down into the streets. The horses bucked and shied as yet more shells from the distant German howitzer guns rained in. Each explosion seemed closer than the last, and even louder than before. I could hear the rumbling of collapsing walls. Men shouted. Women and children screamed.

I had no idea what to do! The doorway was certainly no place to be. I made a spur-of-the-moment decision. A covered wagon had drawn up at the kerb beside me. The horse was panicking and the driver had dismounted to fiddle with its harness before he moved off again. I thought that if I stayed where I was I would certainly be killed. Hitching a lift would be better than running! While he tried to soothe the poor animal, I hauled myself up into the cart among its cargo of groceries, still clutching my two loaves. As if it would keep me safe, I covered myself with a smelly blanket from a pile that was lying there. I heard the frightened driver tell the horse to "giddy-up" and found myself being bumped away from the confusion and dust at an unsteady gallop. Peeking out

from under the covering, I could just make out the scars that were beginning to appear on the ancient and lovely face of Ypres. A corner of the Cloth Hall had been completely blown away. Its windows were broken. Its huge wooden door hung at a crazy angle from one hinge.

Despite the blanket and my overcoat, it was icily cold in the back of the cart. I was shivering, probably from the shock of all that had just happened. I twisted my hands together to get some warmth back into them and tried to slow my breathing down. To calm myself I set out to count slowly to a thousand. *I was still alive, wasn't I?* Looking back now, what a clever and brave little girl I was! Yes, but how silly and stubborn too… as you're about to hear.

★

My name is Annette. When all this happened I was just nine years old. I'd always been small for my age, but my legs and arms were strong. I had short fair hair which I liked, and freckles which I didn't. My dad was an Englishman who ran away from home to find his fortune in far off countries when he was sixteen years old. He got no further than Belgium. To his surprise, he found that his name – *Albert Martin* – worked just as well in French as it did in English. The spelling stayed the same: they just said it differently. He must have had a very quick ear, because he was soon speaking French too – with only the slightest accent. As you probably know, Belgium is a country with two languages, but he found himself among French-speaking people, and he never really got to grips with Flemish. It probably didn't help that within a year or so he'd met my mother, Elise, and before long they were sweethearts. *Her* Flemish wasn't very good either. Once they were married, my brother Michel came along quite quickly, and I followed two years later.

Dad was a blacksmith, and he was always at his happiest working in the heat and sweat of his forge, bending hard iron to his will. His customers loved him.

"You're a genius, Albert," they would say. "Is there *anything* you can't make?" And he would smile shyly, and accept their generous tips with a touch of his cap.

After they married, my parents moved to the city of Antwerp, which is where we spent my happy early childhood years. Then, in 1913, it was on everyone's lips that war was coming. I can remember Dad saying to Mum as we sat at the kitchen table, "It *will* happen, Lizzie. It's just a question of when. The Germans will want to get their hands on Paris, and Belgium's in the way. If we're smart we'll make our exit while we still can."

"But where to, Bertie? Where?" she replied with big eyes, smoothing her long hair away from her face. "You'd never go back to England, would you now?"

And he'd looked up at her solemnly from beneath his dark fringe, shaking his head sadly in agreement. He'd always said he'd left England for good. It would be a total failure to turn up like a bad *centime* in Witney, and have to start again.

In the end we *did* make a move, but a shorter distance to just outside the city of Ypres. My grandpa had died when I was very small, and my mum was his only daughter. Now Grandma had become ill. She was just about surviving on the family farm, but it was going to rack and ruin around her. Her mind had gone.

"This place is disgusting," Mum had whispered when we first arrived. "It's more fit for an animal than a human."

Grandma couldn't even feed herself properly, and there was no one close by who cared enough to help. So we'd packed up our nice life in Antwerp and moved east to the little village of Maninghem, five kilometres from Ypres. I didn't like it there. Grandma was really very difficult, and my mother was usually tired and cross. She was always yelling, particularly at me. Despite my small size, I'd been born with a strong will. I could never take "no" for an answer. I made up stories too. They entertained me, and I think I even half-believed some of them. I would rattle on about ghosts I'd seen, or rabbit-sized rats, or unlikely people I'd met in the lane. The stories didn't amuse Mum one bit.

"You're a bad girl, Annette. And you'll come to a sticky end. I can't ever trust a thing you tell me," she would shout, as she smacked my legs and bottom. Her smacks stung and so did her words. I didn't think I deserved them.

Dad wasn't happy either. The farm was hard to organize and control. Every day he felt he was losing a battle with nature.

There was precious little time free to spend in his workshop, apart from mending tools that broke in the difficult ground. And all through the autumn of 1914 it seemed as if any minute we'd have to abandon the farm. Just a few miles away thousands of soldiers from the German and British armies were digging deep trenches. During the previous few months they'd chased each other backwards and forwards over most of Holland and Belgium. But now the ground was slowly becoming sticky with mud. Soon it would be hard enough just walking across the fields, let alone moving heavy guns over them or carrying a heavy pack.

"They'll not go anywhere before the spring now," my dad said. "Perhaps we'll be all right for a while. And anyway, this war isn't *about* anything. Surely the politicians will see sense soon."

I'm sixteen years old now. The nine-year-old Annette of 1914 constantly amazes me. She might have been naughty and a storyteller, but I think she was much braver and more confident than I am. How on earth did I cope when Dad and Michel disappeared that dreadful October day? When I think about it, a wave of sadness washes over me.

It had been another horrible wet morning after a glorious early autumn. The two of them were soaked through before they'd even started, yet they still waved a cheery goodbye to Mum and me as they traipsed off to help fix the fences in a neighbouring village. They never came back. I still hope that one day I'll see them again, but in my heart of hearts I know I won't. Not unless the priest is right and we all meet again in heaven some day.

What happened to them? Well, I used to wonder if they'd been taken prisoner by the Germans. More likely they were shot by one side or the other. Maybe someone thought they were soldiers. But how could anyone mistake my eleven-year-old brother, Michel, for a soldier? He could scarcely pick up a rifle, let alone shoot one.

CHAPTER TWO

So that's how I came to be in the centre of Ypres, trying very hard not to get killed by the Germans. The driver of the wagon I'd climbed into was now pushing his horse and cart along at breakneck speed, and who could blame him? The wagon pitched and rolled. The horse whinnied and bucked as it felt the whip bite into its flanks. The driver swore loudly and often. I thought we'd end up in a ditch. Between the canvas covers at the rear of the cart I could see we were moving out of the town. From the direction of the sun I thought we might be heading north-east. It was a part of Ypres I didn't know, and a horrible thought suddenly struck me. I'd assumed that the driver was a true Belgian and on our side, but for all I knew, he might be taking food to the *Germans*. I had no idea exactly where the front lines were, or if there were ways of crossing from one set of trenches to the other. I thought to myself that if the wagon ever came to a halt, I should hop out and make a run for it, but nothing ever seemed to get in our way.

I can't say how long it was before the pace slowed, the cart stopped moving and I began to hear the chatter of voices around us. It felt as if we'd been on the road for hours, but thirty minutes was probably more like it. I held my breath and listened carefully. To my great relief the voices were speaking English. Then the canvas covers at the rear of the wagon were pulled fully open, the sun streamed in, and someone said, "Well, bless my soul. What 'ave we got 'ere?"

My eyes were blinded for a few seconds, but then I found I could make out the shapes of two men. One was wearing a soldier's uniform. The other was the driver.

The driver swore in French and said roughly, "What's your game? You little rascal! Fancied stealing a few groceries, eh?"

He reached in and pulled me out of the cart. I fell into his chest and, probably because I was in a state of shock, completely lost my temper. I went at him like a mad dog, banging my fists against him, screaming, scratching and biting. He tried to hold me back by gripping my wrists. The English soldier just laughed.

"Your daughter's a bit fiery, *monsieur*. We should set her on the Huns and see how they like it."

"She's nothing to do with me," the driver hissed. "I haven't the faintest idea where she came from. She must have caught a ride somewhere in town." He was still fending me off. "Ow! You look after her!"

He threw me at the soldier, who caught me neatly and wrapped me up against his greatcoat, pinning my arms so that I couldn't move.

The driver sucked at the wound on his hand where my teeth had sunk into him. He looked at me angrily and spat on the ground. Then with a bad grace he banged his boxes of produce down in front of the soldier.

"That's all for today, Corporal Warren," he growled. "I'll be back tomorrow and we can settle up then. I'm off to Ypres to see if the wretched Germans have left one brick on top of another."

"Bad up there today, is it?"

The driver shrugged his shoulders. "More

shells than before. Bigger bombs. Even using one of those newfangled flying machines. We're at their mercy, unless your lot can do something about it. Why do you think I sell to you and not them?"

"What about the girl? You're taking her back with you?" the corporal asked. The driver swore again. "You must be joking," he said, with a coarse laugh. "Think of her as part of today's delivery. You deal with her!"

And before the soldier could argue, he whipped the canvas covers back across the back of the wagon, heaved himself into his saddle and kicked his old nag into a trot, waving a rude goodbye over his shoulder as he went.

"Oh good," said the soldier to himself. "So what am I supposed to do with you?" He called across the yard in which we were standing. "Oi, Perkins! You seem to have time on your hands. I need you here. Now, private soldier. Not tomorrow morning."

"What's your name?" Private Perkins asked me gently. I told him it was Annette, and he said his was Charlie. "And how old are you?" I answered that I was nine.

Charlie was very young — too young to shave — and slimly built. A mop of unruly dark hair poked out from inside his soldier's cap. He was the first person who'd smiled at me all day.

"What about brothers and sisters?"

Thinking about Michel, I began to cry. And to my surprise his eyes filled up with tears too.

He took a handkerchief from his pocket. It was none too clean but he wiped my cheeks and then his own.

"Don't let the corporal see," he said with another smile. "That would never do. He'd have me cleaning the latrines for not behaving like a proper soldier. I know all about missing family. I've got a wheelbarrow full of brothers and sisters. I write letters, but God knows whether they ever reach home. Leastways, they never write back, even those as can."

I looked around me. We were in the stable yard of what was probably a fine house. There were low buildings on all sides of the yard's cobbled floor, some of them open at the front. We were sitting on two low canvas chairs in one of the barns beside a stove which pumped heat out into the chilly morning. On the corners of the buildings rose bushes climbed the walls. Charlie saw me looking.

"The house is called *Les Roses*," he said, "Because of the flowers, I suppose. We call it '*Rosie*'."

"Do the owners still live here?" I asked.

"Long gone," he answered. "Took what they could carry, and fled to England. You speak very good English for such a little girl! How's that then?"

I explained about my dad.

"So where are your family now?" he asked.

What I did next seems dreadful to me now. Without a moment's hesitation I told the biggest fib of my life.

"They're all dead," I answered. "My dad,

my brother, my mum. All of them. Our farmhouse was blown up by a German gun."

Charlie looked stunned. "How did you escape?"

I thought quickly. "I was down the garden in the privy. And then I ran away."

What a whopping, terrible lie! But can you see why I might have told it? Since the Great War ended, people know that soldiers sometimes become 'shell-shocked'. Their minds get scrambled by the awful things they've seen in battle and they go to pieces. Maybe that's what happened to me in Ypres. Even as I was sitting there with Charlie I'd become more and more cross with Mum every minute. Surely she'd known the city was too dangerous? The driver of the wagon had just made it perfectly clear. Ypres had been bombed before. And if Mum had known that, what possessed her to send me in to buy bread? Even Madame P. had been surprised. I could have been killed. So now, if Michel and Dad were never coming back, what did it matter if I pretended to have lost Mum and Grandma too? Hadn't Dad run away from home when he wasn't much older than me?

Charlie could see I was shivering. "I think we could both do with a mug of something hot," he said. "Just hang on a mo'."

He fetched a tin billy-can and some water, and used a stand made from twisted wire to heat up the billy over the stove. From his pocket he produced some paper wraps containing a sticky dark brown substance, which went into the water.

"Oxo..." he smiled, "...beef tea. You'll like it. Makes everything seem better."

He was right. It was comforting to hold a hot drink and inhale the meaty aroma.

However, when I took a sip it tasted vaguely of petrol. I must have wrinkled my nose. Charlie noticed and laughed.

"I know," he said. "I'm sorry. It's those flimsies – the cans we store the water in. You'll get used to it. It doesn't seem to do us any harm. And the sergeant says we've got to keep drinking plenty, otherwise we'll be fit for nothing."

While I'd been in the wagon, I'd stuffed half a stick of bread into my coat pocket and, despite my little fight with the corporal and the driver, it was still there. I pulled it out, and offered some to Charlie.

"Well, thank you young lady, I don't mind if I do," he laughed. "Share and share alike! You've got to take it where you find it, I always say."

As we talked, the sun moved round the angle of the roof and streamed into the barn. What with the tea and the stove and the additional heat from the sun, I quickly went from being chilly to drowsily warm. I'd been up before six: it had been a long and dramatic morning. Charlie's voice was low and soothing, and I fell asleep where I sat.

I must have slept for several hours, because when I woke the afternoon light was already beginning to fade. The soldiers had moved me and I was now lying on a camp bed covered with a coarse blanket. Charlie was nowhere to be seen, but around me there was a pleasant hum of activity. The smell of cooking drifted towards me from one corner of the yard. Men were queueing by a cart. From behind the cart two women in uniform were dishing out something brown and sloppy onto tin plates. The soldiers ate greedily, laughing and joking as they scooped up mouthfuls of food and wiped their dirty mouths on their sleeves. From the other side of the courtyard came the snort and stamp of horses. Two fine-looking mares were being brushed down while a patient old carthorse stood next to them with one leg raised, having a shoe replaced. A lorry had arrived at the entrance to the yard, and lengths of board and rolls of chicken wire were being unloaded under the corporal's beady eye. A few metres away, a row of men were carefully cleaning their rifles, pulling lengths of cloth through the gun-barrels. Immediately next to me a soldier with carrot-red hair was sitting in his vest peering at his army jacket. He had a clown's face with a squint and a broken nose. In his left hand he held a candle. He ran the candle up and down the seams of the jacket, one by one. He caught me watching him and laughed.

"Don't you mind me, missy," he chuckled. "It's the lice, see. The little critters likes to hide where you can't see 'em. But a candle'll always find 'em out, don't you worry. Like

…that!" And he pounced on something with a thumb and forefinger, squashed it, and rubbed his finger in the dirt beside him.

"Don't you just wish to blazes the flippin' Hun could be so easily squashed, eh? I'm Ginger, by the way. Charlie's mate."

I thought he was funny and sat up so that I could watch more closely. "Oi, Charlie," Ginger hollered. "You're needed over 'ere." And then I saw Charlie coming through a gap in the walls followed by a tall, slim, smartly dressed officer. They were talking. When Ginger saw the officer with Charlie, he added with another shout, "Begging pardon, sir". Charlie waved a hand in our direction either to show he'd heard or perhaps to shut Ginger up. He finished his conversation with a salute and crossed the yard towards us.

"I hope Private Phipps here isn't getting you into mischief?" he said, smiling.

"As if I would," Ginger replied. "I'm shocked you should ever dream of such a thing, Private Perkins."

"Now, Miss Annette, you could probably do with a wash and brush up," said Charlie, all business-like. "I've had a word with the captain, and he's fine for you to use the facilities in the house. Come with me and I'll show you."

"He's a good lad, is Charlie," Ginger called out as Charlie took me away. "Not like some. He'll look after you all right, miss. And if he gets put upon for something and can't be found, you call on me or the corporal. We're family men with daughters or sisters back home 'bout the same age as you."

*

Les Roses was a handsome building of three stories with four large sash windows on each side of the steps which swept up to its gracious front door. There was a strong smell of polish around the hallway from the wood panels and banisters, but where there was paint, it was chipped, and the paper on

the walls above the stairs was beginning to peel. It was a soldiers' house now. Rough and ready would do.

"There's a toilet and bathroom just here," said Charlie, opening a door at the top of the first flight of stairs, and then closing it again. "And tonight, because no one can think what to do with you yet, the captain says you should sleep in here..."

The room we entered was more grand than any I'd ever slept in. The wallpaper was a beautiful pink and the bed linen was crisply white and deep red. The curtains were heavy and came together with a satisfying swish when the cord was pulled. The bed was so high off the ground I had to clamber up onto it. Charlie handed me a key.

"When you go to bed, lock the door so you won't be disturbed," he said. "No one will bother you unless you call."

Suddenly I felt very alone. "Where will you be?" I asked in a small voice.

Charlie cleared his throat.

"I've done a deal with Captain Garvey. He says he's happy for you to stay here until the morning, but in return he needs me to go out with him tonight. I'm good at cutting my way through barbed wire, see. If you were to walk a couple of miles up the road here, you'd find yourself at the beginning of our CTs – that's 'communications trenches' in army-talk. If you were to keep your head down so you didn't get it blown off, then in another quarter-mile you'd find yourself at the front line. There are two lines of trenches dug in facing the Hun, full of mud and water and Lord knows what, and the furthest of the two is the firing trench. Between our trenches and theirs is an area called No

Man's Land, and in the middle of No Man's Land is the barbed wire the Germans have laid down so we can't get at them. Captain Garvey and me – we're going to cut a big hole in the wire, and then our lads can make a raid tomorrow morning to teach Jerry a lesson he won't forget in a hurry."

"It sounds very dangerous," I said.

"Well, I suppose it is dangerous," he answered. "But it's not the first time I've been out there, and I daresay it won't be the last. If you find yourself with time on your hands tonight I won't mind if you say a little prayer though. All things considered, I'd rather be home in Oxford."

I knew all about Oxford. Dad had talked about its beautiful buildings and wide streets. He'd always said he thought Bruges or Ghent in Belgium were the best, but Oxford wasn't half bad.

"My dad's family came from Witney," I said.

"Well, I'm blowed," Charlie replied, shaking his head. "Do they now? Witney eh? I had an auntie lived there once."

For a moment there was a faraway look in his eyes, and for a few seconds I could tell Charlie was back home, warming himself in front of the fire in an Oxford parlour. Charlie recovered himself.

"Now, we'd better find you some grub before I go and put on my make-up."

I looked at him, puzzled.

"We have to cover ourselves with mud so we blend into the landscape and can't be seen. Still, they do say it's good for the complexion. Fine ladies pay quite a lot of money for the pleasure, so I've heard."

Down in the yard again, as the day faded into evening, Charlie found me some stew and a hunk of bread. There wasn't a lot of meat in the stew, but there were plenty of white beans floating around so at least it filled me up. He made me drink some more petrol-flavoured tea, and then said, "Right, you're on your own till the morning now. There's no one else to boss you about, so I'm going to act like your big brother, and tell you to go and hunker down in that nice room of yours until the morning. Night, night, Annette, and watch the bugs don't bite. Only, out here you know they will! I'll come and see you tomorrow as soon as I can."

In the bedroom I thought to myself, "*But what if Charlie doesn't come back?*" And then I tearfully remembered Dad and Michel. I even spared a grudging thought for Mum, too. She was probably worrying herself silly wondering where I'd gone while she tried to get some food into Grandma. But it was too late now. I'd told my big fib. I couldn't change my story – what would Charlie think of me? And anyway I didn't want to go back to the lonely farm without the protection of my father and brother. I felt very alone and sorry for myself as I wept into my grubby handkerchief.

The sound of a harmonica floated up to my window from the yard, and a quavering voice began to sing:

'There's a lamp that's always burning
Outside a cabin by the sea
And beside its lonely hearth
I know you think of me.
There'll be long, long nights of waiting
Until our dreams come true
And I'm sitting hand in hand
Around that fire with you…'

In the distance I could hear the deep rumble of gunfire. Charlie and I were in for a very long night too.

CHAPTER THREE

In fact I slept very well and I was up with the lark. When I'd splashed some cold water on my face I went down to the yard. Charlie was nowhere to be seen but Ginger Phipps was there.

"Good kip, miss?" he asked. I said it had been. "Glad to hear it," he said. "Now, we're not to worry, and of course I do because he's such a good pal of mine, but we've had a message sent down about Charlie. *He's* OK, but Captain Garvey ain't so clever, and apparently it was a bit of a do getting him home. Charlie'll be along in a while, but he's spent a few hours getting some sleep in a dug-out up near the line. So just you sit tight for a while 'til he gets here."

"What's a dug-out?" I asked. He looked at me, amazed I didn't know.

"Well, I suppose you wouldn't, would you? It's what it sounds like. To make sure the lads aren't open to all weathers up at the front, we dig out a few extra holes in the ground and cover them over. It's amazing what you can do with a length of old corrugated iron and a few lumps of wood. Your dug-out becomes a home away from home after a while. Somewhere to do the crossword when Jerry's not chucking stick-bombs or doing his best to knock your head off."

It was a long hour or two before Charlie arrived. He hobbled into the yard, covered in mud from head to toe, carrying a pack that looked far too heavy for one man. A few of the soldiers turned and gave him a cheer. He dropped the pack and sank down on a bench.

"Seems your Private Perkins is a bit of a hero," remarked Corporal Warren, as he walked past. "Comes as something of a surprise to me, I must say. You're obviously a good influence on him, young lady."

A little knot of men had gathered around Charlie. Like the nosey girl I am, I went over.

"Well, make room for my lucky charm," said Charlie, beaming at me. "Am I glad to see you!"

"Tell us the gory details, Chas," said one of the men. "How did it go?"

"Not much to say, lads…"

"Not what we heard," said another.

"Well, since you ask," Charlie said, between puffs on a cigarette he'd been handed. "It was black as the ace of spades out there. Couldn't see your hand in front of your face. We made it out into No Man's Land all right, though it was a long old crawl. And then those new cutters of mine started making short work of the wire. Except I'll tell you the strangest thing. Once you start pushing the wire this way and that, with no stars to see I'm blowed if you don't lose all sense what's east or west.

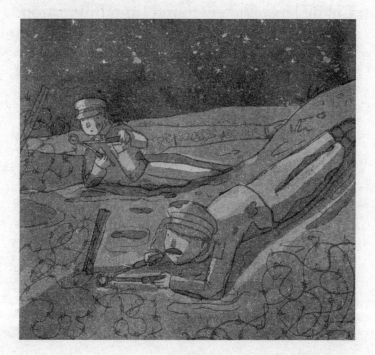

"So you got lost?"

"We could have been anywhere. And it fair gives you the runs when you thinking you're going to end up in one of Jerry's trenches. Pardon me for my soldier's language, young Annette. Then all of a sudden, up goes a flare, and for a moment it's like noon on a midsummer's day. We hear Jerry shouting, and he lets off a few rounds in our direction. Only it's gone dark again so there's precious little chance of them hitting us, or so you'd think. Then suddenly there's a cry from the captain and he says to me under his breath, '*I think I've stopped one in the leg, Perkins.*' I crawl over to him, and best as I can feel he's all right, though it's a bit hard to tell what's blood and what's muck. So I take a deep breath – at least I've got my bearings now I know where the fire's come from, assuming it's Jerry shooting and not us. I tie up Captain Garvey's leg and then I haul him all the way back and over the top into the fire trench. And I reckon that must have taken all of an hour too."

"How's Garvey now?"

"He'll live. Might have been more of a graze than actually stopping one. They've put him on a cart down to the dressing station. They'll fix him up again there."

"So it's back to Blighty for him, and a medal for you?"

"I wouldn't count on either, lads. But it don't half make you feel glad to be alive and back at *Rosie*, I can tell you that. I put it down to our little guardian angel here. I reckon she was the one who saved us."

"Any news about the raid?"

"Well, 'C' company went and had a pop at Jerry first thing. But I don't think it came to much, 'cos of course by now Jerry had got wind something was up. I think the boys in 'C' threw a few bombs and came back again sharpish."

When we were on our own later, Charlie said, "I meant that bit about you being my guardian angel. You get superstitious out here. You keep the same lucky charm in your trouser pocket. You carry the same pages of scripture in your jacket. You start to think your life depends on it. We've been up against it these last few weeks, I can tell you. The generals wanted us to batter Jerry good and hard before winter came on, so we were taking regular turns up at the front, and not catching a wink of sleep. We lost a lot of good men one way or another, killed or maimed. You start thinking about your chances of ever making it to the end of the bloomin' war. And if anything at all good happens you hold onto it tight. So maybe you really are my lucky charm, Miss Annette. Only thing is, Corporal Warren says I must take you down to Transport, so they can decide where to send you."

I'd only known Charlie twenty-four hours, but now the thought of moving on without him was scary. I knew it wasn't very safe at *Rosie* – we were so very close to the German lines – but I didn't want to leave Charlie behind. He'd been so kind. He didn't shout or scold. He was my new big brother.

"Can't I stay here with you?" I asked plaintively.

"No, you can't! And you know you can't," he replied. "I've got a job to do. And a very unpleasant one it is. Soldiers aren't fit company for a little lady like you, with all our rude talk and coarse language."

"What's happened to your foot?" I asked,

changing the subject. Charlie was still hobbling.

"Oh, that!" Charlie laughed. "I don't know who made my boots," he said, "but whoever they were, I'd have 'em sacked. The left one started falling apart up at the line, and by the time I'd pulled myself out of a hundred squelchy mud-holes and tripped over a dozen rotting tree-stumps, the sole came off completely. It was slowing me down, so it had to go, and now I hope I can find myself a new one from somewhere. Meanwhile, I'll have to make do with this." And he

 pointed down at the khaki bandage he'd wound round his foot, made from the tight stockings or "puttees" the soldiers wore on their lower

legs for extra support. "But don't you mind about that. Let's go and find the corporal and tell him we're on our way."

The corporal was busy and spoke only to Charlie, not to me. And considering Charlie was now a hero, he spoke rather roughly, I thought.

"It's all very well, Private Perkins, you chasing after the likes of our Captain Garvey and his pet schemes, but I need your mind back on your job. You say the young lady has family in Witney, so if no one's got a better suggestion, you could tell Transport she should be sent there. At least she doesn't come from Penzance or the wilds of Scotland. That might be more difficult for the Oxfordshire regiment to arrange."

I opened my mouth to say something, but Charlie motioned me to keep quiet. I hadn't thought things through. I'd never met any of my Witney family – though Dad had often talked about them. Even if they were willing to take me in, perhaps I'd be no happier than I'd been with Mum and Grandma. As we walked down a lane towards Transport, Charlie said, "Lots of your people have made the journey to England, you know. You won't be the first. From what I've heard half of Belgium's there. A few months back, when we were coming up to Ypres, we passed hundreds of them on the road, poor devils. All they had was what they were stood up in, or could throw on a cart."

I think I must have been whimpering a little as he said this.

"Now then," he said, stopping and turning me round to look at him. "That won't do at all. Let's put on our best face, so we make a good impression."

★

Transport had taken over the offices of a timber yard in a large village a couple of miles from *Rosie*. Next to the yard was the railway station, with a number of sidings containing wagons and carriages. The station buildings had been turned into a hospital. I was shocked to see a long line of men lying on stretchers next to the station door.

One of them was groaning loudly and thrashing around where he lay. A man with a Red Cross badge on his arm ran to him and knelt over him, trying to get him to drink, but the injured soldier knocked his arm away, spilling the contents of the cup. Then I saw that most of his right leg had been blown off, leaving just a stump covered with dirty bloodied bandages. He screamed at the orderly, "For God's sake help me. *Help* me, man. I'm dying…"

"I'm trying," the orderly said calmly. "The drink will make you feel better. But I can't help you if you won't help yourself…"

Charlie pulled at my hand, "Sometimes it's best not to look," he said. "Gets the imagination going too much."

But I'd already seen the pain on the soldier's face and wouldn't forget it in a hurry. And I'd seen the other line of stretchers too, where just the shapes of men were visible under blankets that covered their bodies from head to toe. I didn't want to believe what I saw, but in my heart I knew they were dead.

A train had just arrived in the station and soldiers were milling around the wagons, looking for their packs and sharing a joke. Charlie asked where he could find the Chief Transport Officer. A couple of chaps shrugged their shoulders, but a gangling lad who was doing his best to make the yard tidy with a broom pointed us in the direction of a tall, haughty-looking man with a hooked nose and a wispy moustache.

"You can try Captain Leveson, I suppose. He doesn't take any nonsense, but he knows his stuff."

Captain Leveson was standing outside one of the doors of the offices watching

the chaos. He was tapping his officer's stick impatiently against one thigh and shaking his head. It didn't look a good moment to be asking a favour.

"Private Perkins, sir, 'B' company, 2nd Battalion Oxfordshires. I've been sent to you to ask if you would take this young lady, sir."

"Take her?" Captain Leveson barked impatiently. "Take her where?"

"She's lost her family, sir, who rightly speaking are Belgian people. But she has other family in Witney, Oxfordshire, and my corporal thought that you might be able to help."

"Oh, he did, did he?" the officer snapped.

"How very kind of him! Has he any idea, I wonder, of the difficulties we're working with here?" He spread his hands out towards the crowded yard. "Has your corporal by any chance considered what would happen if I let one small Belgian girl waste His Majesty's time and money by being evacuated hundreds of miles to the middle of England? I suppose I should shortly be overwhelmed by thousands of children presenting excellent reasons why they should be given special treatment too. No, Private Perkins, my compliments to your *corporal*, but please tell him he must return the young lady to the Belgian authorities for them to help her. Have I made myself clear? Now, if you'll excuse me…"

And he strode away, his stick under his arm.

"Now that's what I call a jumped-up, self-important little toff," said Charlie to the captain's back. "If I'd known I was going to be working for the likes of him, I'd have thought twice about volunteering for foreign service. Well, we're for the high jump now. Corporal Warren isn't going to like Captain Leveson's message one little bit. But I can't see anything for it – it's back to *Rosie* for us."

The idea of Witney had given me cold feet, so secretly I wasn't too unhappy about that. And I got the impression Charlie felt the same way. After all I was his "lucky charm". As we were about to go out of the yard gate on our way back to 'B' company, Charlie said, "Just hang on here a mo', Miss Annette, I've had a thought," and he limped away towards the station building. Ten minutes later he was back. This time he ran easily across the yard, kicking his feet up in the air like a dancer as he came.

"At last the old horse is properly shod," he said. "Just have a look at these new boots. Fit like a glove. Much better than the old ones."

"Where did you get them?" I asked innocently.

He tapped his nose, "Well, let's just say they were a present from someone who doesn't need them anymore."

I didn't understand. "You mean a wounded soldier…"

Charlie looked sheepish. "Well, not wounded as such. More sort of… permanently out of action."

I still looked puzzled.

"Passed away?" Charlie explained. "Pushing up the daisies?"

And then I got it. It seemed shocking to me that Charlie should be so happy walking around in a dead man's shoes, so as we trudged the road back to *Rosie*, Charlie chatted away while I listened. Puttees were all very well for keeping your trousers from flapping about, he said, but the lads agreed they cut off the circulation.

"And word is," he added, "when you're up to your knees in water every day for a week and your feet are rotting away, they only make the problem worse. 'Trench foot' they call it."

The sides of our road home were broken

by shell-holes that were now half-filled with water. The surface of the road was a patchwork of repairs.

"That's from when we chased the Germans back over the canal a couple of months ago," he said. "They tried blowing up the road to make it harder for us to catch them."

On the muddy grass outside *Rosie's* stable yard, a game of football was being played. Charlie gave a yelp of pleasure.

"It's our lads against the Frenchies from near Messines," he cried. "I did hear mention they'd fixed up a match."

We stood and watched for half an hour as the war was forgotten. The goalposts were piles of coats. The heavy ball had seen much better days. It was coming unstitched and wasn't really round anymore. After a while one of the English players shouted to Charlie,

"See you've found yourself some new boots, Chas. Well, I'm about done, so come and put 'em to good use!"

"Excuse me, miss," Charlie said, "But a fella's got to do his duty for King and Country." He whizzed around the pitch, running from side to side at full tilt and never getting anywhere near the ball. Where did his astonishing energy come from? Charlie reminded me so much of Michel. He'd been exactly the same.

As the game was drawing to an end, we heard the sound of an engine puttering towards us high in the sky. Everyone stopped and looked to the east. Against the backdrop of the grey clouds could be seen the fat cigar shape of a long balloon.

"By God, it's a Zepp," someone shouted. "Shoot the blooming thing down."

"Better to take cover," cried someone else. Not waiting to find out if they were about to be bombed, the French soldiers were busy declaring the game a draw. They snatched up their coats and knapsacks, shook hands with the English players and lit cigarettes as they clambered onto the lorry that had brought them there. A handful of English soldiers ran out of the stable yard and aimed their rifles at the Zeppelin. They let loose a round or two but then gave up. The balloon was well out of range.

"Taking snapshots of us, I wouldn't wonder," Charlie said. "So they know where to aim their big guns. Wonders of the modern world, they do say, but I hate Zeppelins with a vengeance. Those German devils have got all kinds of tricks up their sleeve. You hear tell of poison gas and flame-throwers and all kinds of mischief they'll make if we don't finish this war off quickly. What are things coming to?"

At last the great machine wheeled around in the sky and its engine faded into the distance. The excitement over, calm briefly returned to the house. We still had to report to the corporal. As Charlie had guessed, he wasn't best pleased.

"Sergeant major's going to give me a good kicking because of that idiot Leveson," the corporal growled. "I suppose you did your best, Perkins. No offence, miss, but you need to make yourself scarce for the rest of the day while I put this man to proper soldiering. And then tomorrow morning we'll see if there are any policemen left in Ypres who know what to do with you."

"I'm sorry," said Charlie, when we were alone again, "but you heard the corporal…"

"It's all right," I answered, although it wasn't "right" at all. "There are books I can read up in the house."

I let Charlie take me back to my pretty room and for a few hours did what I was told. The rest of *Rosie* was a mysterious dark brown place. As we'd passed the drawing room on our way upstairs, I heard men talking earnestly in low voices. Charlie put a finger to his lips.

"The generals are in there," he whispered confidentially as we climbed towards the bedroom door. "Making life-and-death plans..." He laughed hollowly "...though you can bet your life they won't be the ones who end up dead." I thought it wasn't much of a joke.

He sighed because he hadn't made me laugh and for a moment looked very forlorn. Then he pulled himself up straight. "There now, that's quite enough of that because you're right and it's disloyal talk. You must pretend you never heard me say such a thing.

Let's do as the nice corporal said, and I'll see if I can sneak back to say hello later."

I tried to read, but the books stacked on the bookshelf were dusty and boring. There was nothing to see from the window but roofs and sky. Eventually, I plucked up courage to open the bedroom door. I shut it quietly and tiptoed along the corridor. No one was about. At the end of the passage I found the back stairs and went down. Still no one to be seen or heard. Another flight of stone steps took me round a corner and into a magnificent kitchen. Gleaming pots and pans hung from the walls. Cupboards held mounds of china. Large sinks which had once allowed a team of scullery maids to do the washing-up were now gathering a film of dust.

I was puzzled. Outside in the cold courtyard, I'd tasted what was served up to the soldiers from the carts. Why weren't they using this wonderful old kitchen with its cutlery and kitchen tools?

Two doors led out of the kitchen. I opened the nearer one with difficulty and saw more stairs leading down into a dark, musty cellar. The second door was half-glassed and led from the kitchen to the outside world. There was a key in its lock. I turned it. The door had been well-oiled and it opened easily without a squeak. Beyond was a kitchen garden with a gravel path leading to a gate and empty fields. For a moment I considered abandoning Charlie and *Rosie*. I could escape to the west. I'd be safe if I followed the sun away from the fighting armies. I stepped out of the shadow of the house and was surprised to see a figure hunched down against the wall. It was a soldier, though he looked more like one of the miserable beggars I remembered seeing in Antwerp when I was small. But there was one shocking difference. The soldier's fingers were resting on the handle of a black handgun, which he was pointing at his own right leg, just above the ankle. Huge sobs were shaking the soldier's chest. He didn't look up. Clearly he hadn't seen or heard me.

"I can't do it," he was saying to himself over and over again. "I can't do it. Not anymore. I want to go home!"

I hadn't the foggiest what to do. Even if I tiptoed past him over the gravel path, he'd be bound to hear me, and with a gun in his hand there was no telling what might happen. But it seemed wrong to ignore someone in such a bad way. I wanted to lay a hand on his shoulder and tell him everything would be all right. But I couldn't.

I took the coward's way out. I stepped

back silently towards the door, and squeezed myself into the safety of the kitchen. Almost as soon as I'd carefully shut myself in, there came the sound of a single gunshot. It was followed by a scream of pain that seemed to go on for ever. I put my fingers in my ears and fled back up the two flights of stairs and along the top corridor. Even before I'd left the kitchen, boots were running across the flagstones and gravel outside. Whatever had happened, it was someone else's problem now.

Half an hour later I was still shaking and shivering under the blankets when Charlie knocked on the door and came in. I sat up. He smiled toothily. You'd have thought he didn't have a care in the world.

"Hello, Miss Annette. Been having a nice forty winks, have we?" he said softly.

I said nothing, but I must have looked frightened.

"Hey, what's the matter? Nothing to be scared of. It's only old Charlie, not a blinking ghost. Now, I've come to tell you something."

I nodded feebly.

"I've got to be up and about again tonight. There's a large pile of timber to be carried up to the line … to keep the lads' feet dry. 'B' company have copped for the job."

"I heard a noise," I said, not really paying attention to what he was saying.

"Oh, that…" Charlie was trying to sound casual. "That was nothing."

"I heard a shot from a gun. There was a man…"

Charlie gave me a funny look.

"What man? Has someone been bothering you?"

"The man outside…"

Charlie sat down on the end of the bed.

"Oh … that man," he said, looking serious. "You mean little Joe Thorp? How did you hear about him? Look, sometimes … it can all get too much, you know? In a war things can easily get on top of you. Just imagine. You're hundreds of miles from home. You've seen stuff no one should be expected to see, so you get scared. Or worse, you go completely bonkers. So you mistakenly think you can buy yourself a boat ticket back to England with a revolver. There's plenty will say Joe took the coward's way out. Though Lord knows, it takes courage to shoot yourself in the leg, don't you think?"

I nodded again, even more uncertainly.

"So let's not think about that poor old chap, or the troubles he'll face at the court martial once they've put his leg back in one piece. You stay here like a bug in a rug. I'll see you tomorrow. And I'll ask the nice sergeant major to keep a special watch out, so that you're not spooked by any more noises. Remember, you're my lucky girl, so just keep saying your prayers for us all. While you're safe up here, nothing can go wrong. Can it?"

I snuggled into the blankets and let him go.

CHAPTER FOUR

These days anything that happens around the house at night wakes me. I hear the wind moving the branch of a tree against a window, or the creak of floorboards when someone gets out of bed to use a chamber-pot, and I sit bolt upright and catch myself wondering if a burglar has broken in and we're all going to be murdered in our sleep. It all goes back to that night in 1914.

What woke me sometime before dawn the next morning must have been the swoosh of the incoming shell seconds before it landed. I swear I actually saw the blue and yellow flash from the first explosion light up the room.

I felt the pressure on my ears and heard the terrifying, ear-splitting thump as it blew out the window glass onto the bedclothes. I leapt out of bed, felt for my coat where I'd put it on a chair, and pulled the belt tightly around my waist. There were spare candles and matches on the mantelpiece. I grabbed them and lit one of the candles just as a second shell slammed into the far side of the house, rocking the whole building and jarring my teeth.

I threw open the bedroom door and ran across the house down to the kitchen as fast as the flickering flame of the candle would allow. I opened the cellar door and hurled myself downwards, twisting my ankle as I misjudged the last steps to the cellar floor. Even below ground level, the dull explosions were loud enough to rattle the wine bottles in the racks that surrounded me. It was Ypres all over again. I huddled myself against the damp wall. I thought about the poor soldier and his revolver. "*This time,*" I said to myself, "*you really are going to die, Annette. And down here, they'll never find you.*"

After a few minutes in the shadows of the cellar, I slowly pulled myself together, and started to count the bottles of wine by candlelight. If I remember rightly there were three hundred and thirty-one. Well, I had to do something to take my mind off the gnawing fear which gripped me as the explosions continued overhead! I took some of the bottles out of their racks, and blew off the dust. I looked hard at the labels and tried to memorize each one. I put the bottles back and then tried to say out loud a list of the French villages where the wine had been made. I counted the rows of the bricks from the floor to the top of the cellar vault, and down the other side to the floor again. I paced up and down the length of the cellar to try to keep myself warm. End to end it was a hundred and twenty-five paces. I sang myself songs at the top of my voice.

And at long, long last the explosions above me stopped. Suddenly I felt very hungry and thirsty. The second of my candles was burning down, and I thought that I couldn't bear to be alone down there in the dark any longer.

The cellar door at the top of the steps was still ajar, so I crept out into the house, terrified about what I might see. The kitchen at least still seemed to be in one piece. The broad sunny daylight streaming through the window caught thousands of speckles of dust in its beams. The clock said ten o'clock. I watched it for a few moments to see if the hands still moved. They did, but how could I know if the clock was right or not? I was beginning to lose all sense of time. I wasn't even sure now how many days I'd been at *Rosie*. I took a glass, ran the kitchen tap into the sink for a few moments, and poured myself some water. Even after the bombing, a blackbird was singing joyfully in the sunshine of the kitchen garden. Some things stayed the same, despite the war.

I plucked up courage and made my way through the house to the stable yard. It was a mess. The buildings to one side, where the food had been served and the horses shod, were now just a pile of rubble. By the gateway the road had disappeared into a gaping hole. Judging by the spades and picks which lay beside it, a start had already been made on its repair. Across the yard an officer faced a line of maybe forty soldiers. They were a sorry sight, dirty and exhausted, but they were standing to attention as best they could. I could pick out Ginger by the hair poking out from under his army cap, but I couldn't see Charlie. One by one, in alphabetical order, the officer was shouting their names.

"Mountford…"

"Sir," the private soldier answered.

"Newell…"

"Sir!"

"Perkins…"

No answer came. The officer looked along the line of men, and then back at his list. I looked across at Ginger. His head was bowed. My heart missed a beat. In that moment, I knew something was badly wrong.

"Pickles?"

"Sir!"

"Rogers…"

The officer continued with the list. Other soldiers failed to answer to their names too. Smithson and Varley were both missing. At "Wainwright", the captain dropped his voice to finish the roll-call. His eyes avoided his men's, and he said sombrely, "I think I should ask the padre to say a few words."

A tall stooping man came forward. He wore army uniform, but no hat. A clergyman's collar was visible at his neck.

"Today your company has lost some of its best men," he began, "And you have lost some of your best and most faithful pals." My chest and stomach tightened. My eyes began to fill with tears. This was going to be about Charlie. I knew it. "They volunteered to fight for their King and Country in a foreign place when they could have stayed at home in safety. They laid down their lives for their friends. They have done a great thing, and now, lads, we know we must honour their names by continuing to fight the Hun with all our might, so that these brave men will not have died in vain. I call them men, but like some of you they were really just boys of eighteen or nineteen years. But by their courage and comradeship they showed themselves to be truer men than most. Let us now bow our heads and pray that God will give us strength for our tasks as he takes them into His Eternal Kingdom."

The soldiers took off their caps as the padre prayed. I couldn't hear what he said for all the sad, confused thoughts buzzing around in my head. As they finished by reciting the Lord's Prayer together, I let out a wail of anger and despair which echoed around the yard.

They must have let Ginger fall out of line, because the next thing I knew he was kneeling beside me.

"Let's you and me find somewhere quiet for a mo'," he said softly. Taking me by the hand, he led me round a corner to a private spot where an old garden seat still caught the morning sun.

"Is Charlie dead?" I asked.

"You're a big brave girl, and I'm not going to tell you no fibs," said Ginger, kneeling in front of me. "Charlie's not coming back."

He stopped. His chest heaved. For a few moments he was unable to speak.

"I'm sorry," he said eventually. "Charlie was the dearest friend to me."

He wiped a dirty sleeve across his eyes and nose.

"What happened?" I said in a small voice.

"We don't know ... not the whole story,"

he answered. "We were taking the boards and supplies up to the boys in the front line all last night, backwards and forwards, trying to make 'em a bit more comfortable. It was bloomin' hard work, I don't mind telling you, because it was so dark. We were stumbling around and falling over and hitting each other on the head with the planks." Ginger had a spectacular black eye. "Then the cloud cleared. We didn't know the dirty Hun had been planning to hit us so hard."

"The Zeppelin…" I began.

"Well that was probably part of it," Ginger answered. "Just before first light, while they were giving you hell down here at *Rosie*, what seemed like the whole Jerry army came over the top and through the wire straight at us. I was one of the lucky ones 'cos I was well on my way back home at the end of the shift. Corporal Warren says Charlie was still up near the line. He reckons a grenade caught him at the top of the communication trenches, and probably Smithson too. They know Varley copped a sniper's bullet. The silly so-and-so never could keep his head down. We told him a thousand times that if you're six foot and something tall in your stockinged feet, you've got to bend your knees or you'll be a certain goner. Up the line, 'C' company lost half a dozen lads, and another ten wounded. The miracle was, between us all we gave the Hun a very bloody nose. They've been clearing Jerry corpses out of the way all morning."

"Where's Charlie now?" I asked.

Ginger looked away and said nothing.

"So I can't see him?"

"Best not to ask," he croaked. "Truth is, there might not be anything of Charlie left to see. Even if there was, you wouldn't want to go upsetting yourself."

I began to cry again.

"Try to remember him the way he was," Ginger said gently. "That's what I'll do. He was a lovely lad was Charlie. We were the best of pals. We joined up together, and we trained together on Thetford Heath. Shared a night out on the beer more than once in better times. And then we ended up serving together…" Ginger broke off, turning his face away from me so that I wouldn't see his tears.

"He thought the world of you. Said you were a real bobby-dazzler, and nothing bad could happen because of you turning up the way you did. You'd think we were all hard men what with the things we do and see. But then, underneath the King's uniform, we're all as soft as putty."

I let him be for a few moments, and

then I spoke up in a strong voice that even surprised me, "I want to see where it happened. Will you take me there?"

Ginger turned back towards me, startled.

"I can't do that. They'd have my guts for garters."

"I want to see," I repeated more loudly.

"It wouldn't be safe. Not for you or me."

"It's not exactly safe here, is it?" I sulked. "Life's not very safe. It's only luck I wasn't killed in the house last night. I've lost everyone important to me – my dad, my brother…" I caught my breath. "…my mum and grandma. And now Charlie too. I've got to say goodbye. To him at least."

There was silence. The engine of a lorry revved into life. Somewhere, miles away, the heavy guns kept on rumbling. By the corner of the building there was a large flowerpot with one of the rose bushes that had given the house its name. Against the odds so late in the year, a single stem of red roses showed its face to the sun. I went over to it, and cupped one of the flowers in my hand. Ginger watched me silently.

"All right," he finally agreed. "Look, don't get your hopes up. I'll have a word with the sergeant. We'll see what he says."

CHAPTER FIVE

In half an hour he was back.

"Sergeant Oliver says we can do it, but he's coming too, and so is Corporal Warren. They all had a high opinion of Charlie. The sergeant major's going to turn a blind eye. But if we go, we go now. It's all quiet up there at the mo'. The Germans are having a kip after their early start. And once we're done we come back sharp-ish. You understand, Annette?"

I said I did.

"Can I borrow your knife, Ginger?" I asked.

He pulled it from his waistband, and gave

it to me. I went and cut the stem of roses from the little bush.

What happened next sometimes now seems like a dream, but I promise the four of us really did walk out of *Rosie's* main gate, and up the road towards the lines. It felt good to be outside in the real world again. We strode briskly between fields studded by muddy shell-holes. The trees in the fields and at the roadside were mostly just burned, twisted stumps. Soldiers coming the opposite way gave us the oddest of looks. I was beginning to resemble a street urchin. My brown boots were covered in mud, and the dress of my skirt and my petticoat were grimy with the dirt of three days. Where the road bent away sharply to the right, we dropped down into the field on the left and into a ditch which began to zig-zag its way forward. Sergeant Oliver went first with Corporal Warren in the rear. I walked between them and just in front of Ginger.

"From now on, talk quietly," he whispered. "No point alarming Jerry. Just follow the sergeant."

It was just about possible to pass someone coming from the opposite direction, but sometimes only with difficulty. We were walking on boards similar to ones I'd seen stacked in the yard, presumably the same kind that Charlie had been carrying up to the line last night. We quickly came to a point where one side of the trench had fallen in. Some men were shoring the sides up where they could, and hacking with their tools at the earth to widen the space, or perhaps to start a new trench running at an angle to the old one. As if it were the most natural thing that I should be there, one said, "Hello, me old darlin'. How's it goin'?"

"Am I dreaming," said another, shaking his head, "or are the nurses getting younger every day?"

"Just keep your thoughts to yourself, private soldier," the sergeant muttered gruffly. "And concentrate on the job in hand."

A few yards further on the sergeant ducked down to the left, and I found myself in a small underground cavern. On one side of the floor was a mattress. Two men sat on it, while another lay sprawled with his knees drawn up towards his chest, apparently sleeping. A billy-can of water was boiling on a stove. Some shelves had been cut in the mud and chicken-wire walls, and on them sat a row of dirty mugs and some bottles.

"Welcome to the dug-outs," Ginger said. As he spoke, a rat scurried out of a dark corner across his feet and into the trench outside.

I must have looked surprised, but rats don't worry me. I've spent my life in old barns and workshops.

"Say good morning to Heinrich," laughed one of the men. "Or maybe it's Heinrich's brother. I thought I'd got rid of him for good last night."

"Right," whispered the sergeant. "It's just a few more yards now. Outside is what we call Shaftesbury Avenue, after the street in London. Then we get to a place where lots of trenches run into each other, so we call that Piccadilly Circus. About there is where we reckon Charlie was hit."

We left the dug-out and moved forward to the place the sergeant had described. As we stood there, grim-faced, worn-out soldiers passed by. My three companions removed their caps. Ginger produced a small book from his pocket.

"It was Charlie's favourite," he whispered, his voice breaking. "*A Christmas Carol* by Charles Dickens. He only lent it me yesterday. He said he read it every December, regular as clockwork."

Taking a scraper from the corporal, Ginger hollowed out a space on the edge of the trench, level with his head.

"Keep your arms and head down, private,"

hissed Corporal Warren. "I don't want to lose another good man."

Then Ginger placed the small book in the hollow and filled earth in on top of it, pressing down with the flat of the scraper until the ground was level again.

"Here, Miss Annette. Let me," he said.

And he took the rose stem I was clutching and placed it over the spot where the book now lay hidden.

"Charlie Perkins. We'll never forget you," he said carefully.

And as if we'd rehearsed it we echoed his words. "Charlie Perkins. We'll never forget you."

And I never have. I don't think a single day passes without me remembering him. Charlie. My hero.

If I were you, I'd be hoping for a happy ending to this story. Even now, I occasionally see a figure on the street or in the market and my heart skips a beat. Just for a second

I think it's Dad, or Michel, or Charlie, but it never is. None of them are ever coming back. Dad always used to say that every cloud has a silver lining. Somewhere up in the sky the sun still shines even if we can't see it. So let's be sunny for a while and not dwell on the sad things.

★

I spent one more night at *Rosie*, and then early the next morning a woman called Miss Bell announced herself in my room. She wore a khaki-brown jacket and a khaki riding skirt under her greatcoat. With her cap planted on top of her solid square head, she looked just like a woman soldier, but she wasted no time in telling me that actually she was a FANY, a member of the First Aid Nursing Yeomanry. Miss Bell was a lot kinder than she looked or sounded. With her she'd brought a suitcase. Inside was a selection of clean clothes, some of which fitted me. She insisted I had a bath, and when I'd changed she sat me down and started her questions.

She looked at me very directly and said quite gently, "So, Annette … your family … they're all dead or missing?" I thought hard, and made my decision. I looked her straight back in the eye and said they were.

I couldn't help swallowing hard as I spoke, and wondered if I'd given myself away.

"And I gather you still have relatives in Oxfordshire … in Witney?"

"Yes ma'am," I answered with the greatest politeness. "22 Starmer Street."

My memory has always been very good. I'd only seen the address a handful of times on the back of letters from England.

"And their names?"

"My uncle is Herbert Martin, and he's married to my Aunt Emma."

"And how well do you know your uncle and aunt?"

This time I was honest.

"I've never met them, ma'am." And then I added hopefully, "But I'm sure they'd take me in. They've always said how much they'd like to meet me."

That was true. They'd said so in their letters.

"And do you think of yourself as Belgian or English?" Miss Bell suddenly asked in French. Without missing a beat, I answered, also in French,

"I'm half and half. But what's the point in staying here? There's not much left of Belgium now."

"You speak both languages very well," she replied. "And you seem very mature for your age. How old are you exactly?"

"Nine years and four months."

She thought for a while, and then said, "OK. My instructions are to take you to the English Channel at Le Havre, and then for us to catch a boat to Portsmouth. Once we reach England I'm to leave you with another nurse while I come back to France. How do you feel about living in England, at least for a while? Lots of Belgian people have done the same thing this year…"

"I should be very pleased," I said and as I spoke it felt as if an enormous weight had been lifted from my shoulders.

Two days later, after a painfully slow journey across France by train, I was standing in a wintry but peaceful Oxfordshire. No guns. No soldiers. Just the sound of the wind in the trees and the grass. Was there really a war going on four hundred miles away?

Uncle Herbert and Aunt Emma were happy to take me in, though life with them was very strange at first. They already had three children of their own, all younger than me, and so I had to learn to be an older sister for the first time, looking after the others and teaching them to read. For a few years I went to school too, and then when I was twelve (by which time the family had grown by one) I spent my time at home helping Aunt Emma. I've become an excellent cook, and a good gardener. In a few years' time I think I should like to become a teacher.

Two years ago, after the end of the War, I had a great shock. A letter arrived. It was from my mother, asking if Herbert and Emma knew anything of what had happened to me. Grandma had died the previous summer. The farmhouse was in ruins. The land around it was an unworkable mess. My mother was more or less penniless and at her wits' end.

In the following months, she eventually sold the farm for far less than it had originally been worth, and now she lives in Witney too, in a small thatched cottage she rents from a farmer. She's always been a clever dressmaker, and that's how she makes a living now. She and I live together, and these days we seem to get on with each other, more or less. We don't talk about why I ran away: she never asks and I don't say. Maybe some day we'll be able to share our feelings a little more. Uncle Herbert and Aunt Emma know the truth, but they keep their thoughts to themselves.

Last Sunday was Remembrance Day. There was a big noisy parade outside the church with local part-time soldiers and the Boys Brigade band. At eleven o'clock we all gathered silently in front of the new War

Memorial. As the stone monument was unveiled, a single trumpet sounded the Last Post. It reminded me of the trumpet I'd heard the day I was caught up in the bombing at Ypres. Uncle Herbert had been chairman of the committee which had seen to the building of the Memorial so he read aloud the list of fifty-three names that were written on it. The thirty-seventh name was:

"*Private C.H. Perkins M.C.*"

I was so proud. For his gallantry that day in rescuing Captain Garvey, Charlie had been awarded the Military Cross after his death. For my sake, Uncle Herbert had seen that Charlie was included in our War Memorial, even though he'd been born and lived in Oxford. And now, because I too had been there at Ypres, I stood on a box in front of the whole crowd and read the famous poem by Laurence Binyon:

They shall not grow old as
we that are left grow old:
Age shall not weary them,
nor the years condemn.
At the going down of the sun
and in the morning,
We will remember them...

And as I finished reading I thought to myself,
"*That means you, Michel. And you, Dad. And*
you too, Charlie. Rest in peace, all of you."

HISTORICAL NOTE

There's a story you can find on the Internet which says a little girl really did find her way into the trenches early in the First World War. A soldier discovered her and looked after her for a few days. When he was killed shortly afterwards, it's said that his company sergeant major arranged for the girl to be sent to England. The story gives the soldier's name, but no one's ever been able to find him in army records, or track down what happened to the girl in later life. Perhaps it's a true story and the soldier's name was simply written down wrongly. On the other hand, since the first mention of the story is in an American newspaper, it may have been invented to help persuade America to join the war against Germany.

The First World War became known for a while as "the war to end all wars". Sad to say, it ended nothing at all. Wars still rage in many parts of the world today with results that are just as terrible. And some people would say that the way the First World War finished led directly to the Second World War 21 years later.

It's difficult to know the exact figures, but over ten million people were probably killed. Britain declared war on Germany on 4th August 1914, following the German invasion of Belgium the previous day. The agreement to end the war was signed on 11th November 1918, which is why Services of Remembrance are held on that day each year. Of the ten million dead, nearly 900,000 were British and Commonwealth soldiers. At first the British troops were made up of regular signed-up soldiers and part-time 'territorials'. It was only in 1916 that the government decided it needed to "call-up" or "conscript" men who weren't soldiers at all. By then, despite the dreadful casualties, it was thought you were a coward if you didn't enlist to fight. Sometimes men who were believed to have avoided military service were handed white feathers in the street and abused. Even men who were doing necessary war work at home were unfairly treated in this way. Conscription wasn't always good for the army either. The conscripts were less effective as soldiers because they hadn't been trained as well. They weren't as physically fit and they couldn't fire their guns so rapidly.

My local village is probably typical. There

were no more than six hundred people living there at the time of the First World War but eighteen of the village's young men were killed. Everyone would have felt the loss. If you live anywhere in Britain you'll probably be able to find a local War Memorial that tells a similar story.

An important part of the War, perhaps *the* most important, was fought close to Ypres. For four years the two sides killed each other over the same few miles of land. Still every day at eight o'clock in the evening by the Menin Gate in the rebuilt town of Ypres (or Ieper, as the Flemish signposts say today), there's a ceremony to remember those terrible times. See if you can find any paintings by Paul Nash in the library or on the Internet to understand what war did to the countryside in which the men fought.

The story I've written is set early in the first year of the War. It seems difficult to believe but at that time men on horses were still charging around among the foot-soldiers. But technology was changing the way battles were fought, and these 'cavalry' as they were called became rapidly out of date. Guns became heavier. Ways of using explosives were changing. So for instance, because the war in Belgium and France was fought from trenches, mortar bombs were developed to drop explosives down from a height onto the enemy, and soldier-engineers called 'sappers' dug under the enemy's trenches to blow them up from underneath. Aeroplanes started to be used as ways of gathering information and to drop bombs. In 1915 both sides used poison gas for the first time. The Germans developed flame-throwers. Armoured tanks began to appear on the battlefield.

With a teacher or parent's help, you should now be able to find many diaries which tell about the experiences of soldiers during the First World War. They often make for difficult reading. The conditions under which the soldiers lived for days on end were extreme. Here are a few sentences from the letter of an army chaplain to his local newspaper about life in a 'dug-out':

"I sleep … with a Tommy underneath and another on top, so close that our bodies on the wire netting are touching. If I move or turn over the others get squashed, and if either of them move, I get pushed up or down … We all grope around like the blind as candles flicker weakly and water splashes… Everything is greasy and sticky. This morning my servant collected the drippings

through the roof and I washed my neck. Greasy gas bags, greasy tin hats, leather jerkins to give us some warmth, sandbags full of filth are hung around the walls. Outside is a maze of passages, all underground, all greasy and all wet…"

Back home in England during the War, life was changing. Eventually, so many men were away fighting that women began to do the jobs that had always been seen as "men's work". And when the soldiers came back, though they often wouldn't talk about the War, their experiences had been so terrible many of them felt the world they returned to should be different. They badly wanted to know they could live the rest of their lives in peace. They wanted better working conditions and more money. The right of women to work and vote became more and more important. In some ways it feels as if the truly modern world began in 1918.

Why did the First World War happen? It's a story for another time – and a very complicated one. But mistakes by politicians and generals are part of the sorry tale, and so is bad luck. Greed and ambition are in there too. It all happened a hundred years ago, but one reason history is important is to make sure bad patterns of behaviour and mistakes are never repeated. Travel around Europe seems so easy these days: it's quite likely you've been to France, Belgium or Germany as well as other foreign countries. It seems impossible to think we could ever declare war on a close European neighbour. But it wasn't so different in 1914. An army officer could be fighting at the front in the early morning and having a drink in his London club in the evening, thanks to the railways and a quick Channel crossing by boat. King George V of Britain and the German Kaiser Wilhelm were cousins. Britain traded widely with all the European countries. Foreign art and music were much admired. The first football match between England and Germany took place in 1899. It won't do to say such things could never happen again. Each generation – and that means you and your classmates one day soon – has to take on the responsibility of making sure there's never another war in Europe.

Glossary

Battalions

Depending on where his home was, each soldier belonged to a 'regiment', in the case of Charlie, the 'Oxfordshire and Buckinghamshire Light Infantry'. Each regiment was divided into 'battalions', and each battalion into (usually four) companies of over two hundred men.

Blighty

Soldiers sometimes called England 'Blighty'. A 'Blighty Wound' was an injury serious enough to get you sent back home and away from the war. Perhaps the soldier in the garden was trying to do this for himself. A self-inflicted wound might result in a court martial, and even a death sentence.

Communications Trenches (CTs)

These provided a safe-ish way to get supplies and men to and from the front line. Like most trenches, they zig-zagged so that enemy soldiers would never have a clear line of fire down a long length of trench.

Duckboards

Keeping dry in the trenches was almost impossible, particularly in winter. However, the army knew it was hard for men to fight if they were wet and uncomfortable, so they did whatever they could to protect them from the weather, by means of 'dug-outs' and making the floors of the trenches secure with hardwood planks which had gaps in them to let the water through, known as duckboards.

Fire Trench

This was the trench nearest the enemy, from which the soldiers fired their guns.

Flare

A firework launched from a special gun to show that someone was in distress or to give light for a few moments on the battlefield. This was usually done so that enemy soldiers could be spotted or fired at. Sometimes known as a 'Verey light' after the man who invented it.

Howitzers

Howitzers are field guns capable of firing shells a number of miles. The biggest German guns could reach targets over seven miles away.

Jerry

The British troops had all kinds of nicknames for German soldiers. One was 'Jerry', but the Germans were also called 'Boches' or 'The Huns' or 'Fritz'.

Mortar

Mortar bombs are big close-range guns, fired from a steep angle. For that reason they were very effective in trench warfare.

No Man's Land

This was the area between the Allied (meaning British, French and Belgian) and German trenches. It could be hundreds of metres in width or just a few. Both sides put up barbed wire between the lines to prevent the enemy attacking, and sometimes landmines were laid for the same reason. It could often be very difficult to get bodies back from No Man's Land when soldiers had been killed there.

Oxfordshires
Six battalions of the Oxfordshire and Buckinghamshire Light Infantry fought in Belgium and France during the First World War. The 2nd Battalion (which I am imagining Charlie and Ginger belonged to) suffered 632 casualties before Christmas 1914.

Padre
There were army chaplains or 'padres' on both sides during the First World War. In the British army, chaplains didn't carry weapons, but tried to comfort men in times of great difficulty and sadness, as well as helping them with everyday things like writing letters home.

Stick bombs

A kind of hand grenade used by the Germans.

Swagger stick

A stick carried by officers as a way of showing rank.

Tommy

A nickname for an ordinary British soldier.

Zeppelin

Zeppelins were German passenger airships which were converted into bombers during the First World War. Airships were slow, but still dangerous enough to kill about 500 people in Britain during First World War air-raids. Aeroplanes soon replaced Zeppelins, because they were faster and could turn more quickly.

Thank you

With thanks to Northampton Newspapers and Angela Scarsbrook and Penny Wythes of the Northamptonshire Family History Society.